A Tree for Emmy

written by
Mary Ann Rodman

illustrated by
Tatjana Mai-Wyss

PEACHTREE
ATLANTA

For Rob, Pam, and especially Emme Wells, gardeners and friends
—M. A. R.

For my daughters —"stubborn and strong and a little bit wild"
and Joe, who can appreciate a nice tree
—T. M.-W.

Ω

Published by
PEACHTREE PUBLISHERS
1700 Chattahoochee Avenue
Atlanta, Georgia 30318-2112
www.peachtree-online.com

Text © 2009 by Mary Ann Rodman
Illustrations © 2009 by Tatjana Mai-Wyss

Cover design by Loraine M. Joyner
Composition by Melanie McMahon Ives

Illustrations created in watercolors and collage. Text typeset in Baskerville Infant; title
typeset in Crunchy Taco and designed in Adobe Illustrator CS 11.0.

Printed and bound in Singapore
10 9 8 7 6 5 4 3 2 1
First Edition

Library of Congress Cataloging-in-Publication Data

Rodman, Mary Ann.
  A tree for Emmy / written by Mary Ann Rodman ; illustrated by Tatjana
Mai-Wyss. -- 1st ed.
      p. cm.
  Summary: Emmy loves the mimosa tree in her grandmother's yard and asks
for one for her birthday, only to find that stores do not sell wild trees.
  ISBN 13: 978-1-56145-475-4 / ISBN 10: 1-56145-475-3
  [1. Silk tree--Fiction. 2. Trees--Fiction. 3. Birthdays--Fiction.] I.
Mai-Wyss, Tatjana, 1972- ill. II. Title.
  PZ7.R6166Tre 2009
    [E]--dc22
                              2008036745

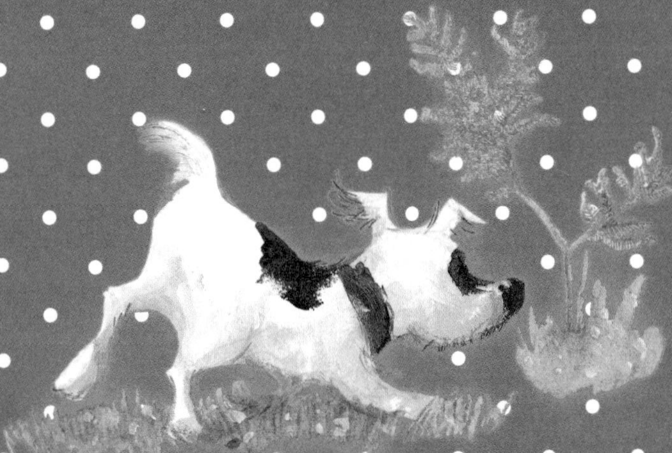

Emmy loved all kinds of trees.

Oak trees with acorns.

Pine trees with cones.

Willows with
long, swishy
branches.

But
best of all,
Emmy loved
the mimosa tree
in Gramma's pasture.

In spring, Emmy swung from the tree's strong, low branches.
"Look at me!" she shouted. "I'm a possum, swinging by my tail."
"I declare, Emmy," said Gramma. "That ol' tree is a lot like you.
Stubborn and strong and a little bit wild."

In summer, the tree was covered with fuzzy pink blossoms.

Emmy put one blossom over each ear.
"Look at me!" she called. "I'm a fuzzy
bug with pink buggy feelers."

In fall, the tree's seedpods covered the ground.
When Emmy shook them, the pods rattled like maracas.

"My tree, my tree, my beautiful tree!" Emmy sang.

She danced around the pasture, shaking the pods.

"Stubborn and strong, and a little bit wild. Just like me."

Emmy's yard didn't have a mimosa tree. It had willows and oaks and pines.

"They're nice," Emmy said. "But they're not stubborn and wild. They're not like me."

Emmy's birthday came in the summer.

"I want a mimosa tree for my birthday," she said.
"What would you do with it?" asked Mama.
"Love it and water it and play with it," said Emmy.
"Okay, then," said Daddy. "Let's go buy a mimosa tree."

But buying a mimosa tree was not so easy.

"A mimosa?" said the man at the garden store. "We don't have any of those."

"Why not?" asked Emmy.

"Mimosas grow wild. We don't sell them."

"Why not?" asked Emmy.

"You don't buy wildflowers, do you, young lady?" said the man. "Stores don't sell clover and dandelions."

"Clover and dandelions are pretty," Emmy said.

"Sorry," said the lady at the next shop. "No one sells wild trees."

"But it's going to be my birthday present," said Emmy.

The lady smiled. "We have plum trees and peach trees, sweetie. They will give you nice fruit."

"But they don't have fuzzy pink flowers," said Emmy.

"Here is a tulip tree," said the lady. "It has lovely pink blossoms in the spring."

"Are they fuzzy?" asked Emmy.

"No," said the lady.

"Do they have rattly seedpods that shake, shake, shake?" asked Emmy.

"No," said the lady. "Pink fuzz and seedpods make a dreadful mess. I'm sure your parents wouldn't want that."

"We want what Emmy wants," said Daddy. "Come on, Emmy. We'll find something else for your birthday."

"I don't want something else," said Emmy.

Mama hugged her. "I know, honey, but we can't find your tree right now. Just for today, could you visit Gramma's tree?"

"I guess," sighed Emmy.

At Gramma's, she ran straight to her favorite tree and gave it a hug.

"Dumb old stores," said Emmy. "No mimosas. No fair." She flopped down under the tree and squeezed her eyes shut, to keep in the tears.

Something touched Emmy's nose. She opened her eyes.
A big weed was tickling her face.

No, it wasn't a weed. With that long stem and those
feathery green leaves, it looked like…

Wait a minute… Could it be?

It was a mimosa tree!

Emmy ran to get Mama and Daddy and Gramma.

"My, my," said Gramma, peering down. "That's a mimosa, all right. A baby one, but a tree all the same."

"Can I have it, Gramma?" begged Emmy. "For my birthday? Please?"

"Why, surely," said Gramma.

So Gramma and Emmy set to work. Carefully, they dug up the tiny tree. Emmy wrapped the roots in wet newspaper so they wouldn't dry out. Then they put the mimosa in a big tomato can for the trip home.

Emmy scouted the yard for a special place for her tree.

"Under my window," she decided. "So I can see it
all the time."

Emmy and her parents dug a hole for the little tree.

"I can't wait for fuzzy pink flowers and rattly seedpods,"
said Emmy. "When will that be?"

"Emmy, honey, it's just a baby tree," said Mama. "It won't have flowers or pods for quite a spell."

"It won't?" said Emmy.

"No," said Mama.

"NO FAIR!" yelled Emmy. "Dumb old tree!" She ran to her room and flopped on the bed. She buried her head in her pillow and wished for a tree like Gramma's. Stubborn and strong. And tall.

Ch-ch-ch-vroom.

Emmy sat up and looked out the window.

Daddy was cutting the grass. Soon he would be under her window.

She ran outside. "Daddy!" she shouted, waving her arms. Daddy turned off the lawn mower.

"My tree," said Emmy. "You're going to mow over it!"

"Hmm," said Daddy. "You mean the dumb old tree?"

Emmy looked down at her tiny tree. "It can't help being small," she said. "It will grow some day. If I water it and love it and keep it safe."

"I suppose so," Daddy said. "Why don't we build it a fence?"

So Emmy and her daddy made a stick-and-string fence, all around the tree.

"Now it can grow," said Emmy. "'Til then, I can pick pink blossoms off Gramma's tree."

But some day soon, Emmy
knew her baby tree would
grow up tall. Stubborn
and strong and a
little bit wild.

Just like her.